TEA WITH THE QUEEN

THE BOWDLEFLODES STORIES

written by
Neil Lawson Bal

illustrated by
Lauren Alderslade

I'm Professor Gett.

I care for animals and pets, heading up a gifted team of **brilliant** young vets.

Three will soon be flying with me,
zooming into outer space,
off to Bowdleflode Land,
a truly wonderful place.

The sea is pink, sand bright blue,
like a magical dream.

The hills are made of chocolate,
the clouds are all ice cream.

This land is well known for its incredible features, with deep lakes, HUGE mountains, and astonishing creatures.

Bowdleflodes are always smiling, happy as can be.

They deeply care for wildlife, so of course do we.

I received an invitation,
brought by Postman Sam.

Once there we're greeted by the Queen, a smile upon her face.

"Welcome to Bowdleflode Land! You'll find there's lots to see.

First, sit back and just relax. Enjoy a cup of tea!"

"My faithful butler
Teepot will pour and
cut the cake.

We'll be joined
by Sally,
A BRIGHT GREEN,
MEGA-LONG
SNAKE."

"It's very good to have you here, to tell you what we do.

Let me give you some details about our wildlife zoo.

"Every animal is welcome,
they live in total peace.
We breed endangered species,
so their numbers will increase."

"You'll meet some crazy animals during your short stay, like

LOLLY,

SCALLIWAG,

AND OCAY."

BOISTEROUS BOYSY,

"Thank you, Your Majesty. What an incredible zoo."

I then began to wonder if we could work here too...

After tea was over,
everyone wanted to

DANCE!

On went the music,
and even the animals pranced.

Queen Charlotte, she just loves to bop, says it keeps her fit.

All the Bowdles do it, **ROCKING** to the latest hit!

Then suddenly the King appeared . . .

PROBLEMS IN THE ZOO!

"Professor Gett, please help
with an injured Bowdleroo!"

On went
sterile gloves
to do
a very
tricky op.

We mend
a badly
broken leg.

Now poor
Roo can
hop!

My vets are all excited, now they want to stay...

Would the Queen perhaps agree to help us find a way?

The whole team now realise this is the perfect space to use their rare breed training. What an **AMAZING** place!

Then all too soon time is up.
Back to Earth by rocket!
VETS!
Ready for the flight!

Map's
safely
in my
locket.

Her Majesty, she beckons me
as we say goodbye.

"There's a job. Head of the Zoo.
I think you should apply."

Before we leave,
she asks us to kiss
her magic ring.

Rockets, now at the ready. The engines start to sing. Jet-propelled and speedy with the biggest wings you've seen!

Back to Planet Earth to tell everyone where we've been.

JOIN PROFESSOR GETT AND HIS TEAM OF VETS AS THEY RETURN TO BOWDLEFLODELAND FOR MORE EXCITING ADVENTURES!

Professor Gett is just about to show off his fantastic new invention to Queen Charlotte when there's an emergency in the Wildlife Park!

Rory the Flying Dog needs help, fast!

CAN PROFESSOR GETT AND HIS TEAM SAVE THE DAY ONCE AGAIN?

DESIGN YOUR OWN BOWDLEFLODE & BECOME A BOWDLEFLODER!

Join children from all around the world by submitting your own Bowdleflodes Creative Creature to our website. You'll get your own free webpage and might even find yourself featured on our social media!

You can even buy a range of products with your Create Creature printed on them!

WEBSITE: BOWDLEFLODES.COM

INSTAGRAM: @BOWDLEFLODESAFARI

We look forwards to seeing you and your Creative Creature very soon.

Love and best wishes from Prof. Gett and the rest of the Bowdleflode Gang xxx

First published in 2021

This edition published in 2021
by
Bowdleflodes Ltd.

www.Bowdleflodes.com

Bowdleflodes Ltd.
Southbrook Road, West Ashling, Chichester,
West Sussex, PO18 8DN

Written and designed in collaboration with Hannah Howell

pb: 978-1-8380224-0-2 | hb: 978-1-8380224-1-9